Mary and Her Bucket

Written by **Vicki Cameron** / Illustrated by **Stella Nam**

CARAMEL TREE

Mary Goes Fishing

Mary goes fishing. She takes her red
bucket and her fishing line.

Mary catches four fish. She puts them in her red bucket with water. The fish swim around in the bucket.

"Mary, Mary, what are you doing?" Joey asks.

"I am fishing. I have four fish. One, two, three, four." Mary points at her fish.

"Why are you fishing?" Joey asks. "Are you hungry?"

"No," Mary says. "I am going to sell the fish and buy a new dress with ten ribbons. My new dress will be pretty."

Confused Counting

Joey counts the fish. "One, two, three, four. You cannot buy a new dress with four fish."

Mary smiles. "Yes I can. I have one bucket of fish. I will sell the fish for two coins."
Mary holds up two fingers.

"Then I will buy three white hens. The hens will lay eggs. Four eggs, five eggs, six eggs."

Mary holds up seven fingers.

Joey is confused.

"Then the eggs will hatch and I will have little chickens. I will sell the little chickens for eight coins."

Mary holds up nine fingers. Joey is more confused.

"Then I will buy a dress with ten ribbons."

Mary claps her hands. She is happy.

SNAP! SPLASH! FLIP FLOP!

Mary dances and sings around
her red bucket.

I have one bucket of fish to sell
Two coins, Three hens,
Four eggs, Five eggs, Six eggs…

Many little chickens to sell
Seven coins, Eight coins, Nine coins,
Ten pretty ribbons on my pretty new dress.

Mary trips on her fishing line.
SNAP!
The fishing line breaks and falls into the river.

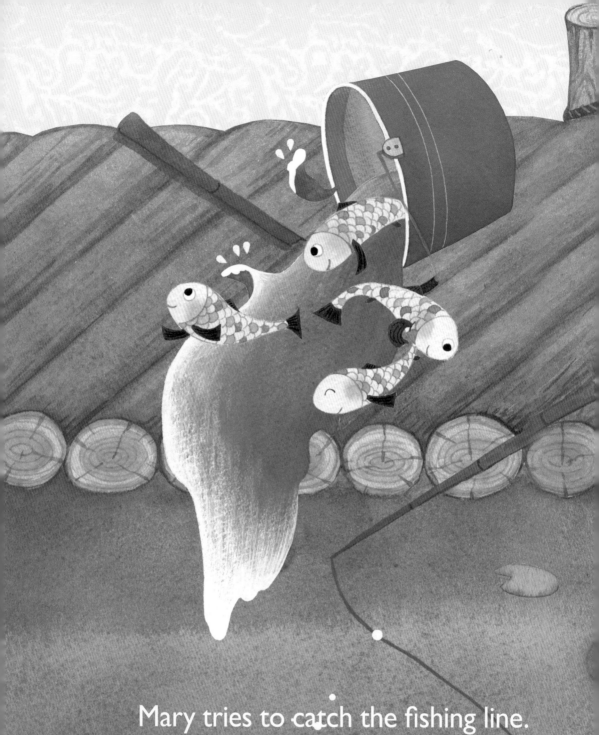

Mary tries to catch the fishing line.
SPLASH!
The red bucket spills over.

The fish fall out.
FLIP FLOP FLIP FLOP!
The fish jump into the river.

Empty Bucket

"Mary, Mary, you have no fishing line," Joey shouts.

"You have no fish." Joey watches the fish
swim away.

"You have no coins. You have no hens. You have no eggs. You have no chickens. You have no new dress. All you have is an empty red bucket," Joey says.

"Mary, Mary. Do not count your chickens before they hatch," Joey says.

Mary is sad.